Hilda Offen

# The Galloping Ghost

Catnip Publishing
HAPPY CAT BOOKS

*For Alison, James and Andrew Currier*

Published by
Happy Cat Books
An imprint of Catnip Publishing Ltd
14 Greville Street
London EC1N 8SB

First published 2008
1 3 5 7 9 10 8 6 4 2



A CIP catalogue record for this book is available from the British Library

ISBN 978-1-905117-66-6

Printed in Poland

www.catnippublishing.co.uk

# Chapter 1

"I don't want to be called Isobel any more," said my sister, striking a pose in the doorway. She was wearing blue lipstick and she'd scrunched up her hair into hundreds of little pink bunches. "I don't want to be called Izzie, either. From now on I want to be known as Bella. It's my stage name."

"Alright, dear," said Mum, looking up from her book. "Bella it is. Bella Weller. Won't that sound a bit odd?"

"I like it!" said my sister. "I think it's dead cool."

That's my sister Izzie all over. She really fancies herself. And since she's been in a band it's got well out of control. She and her friends spend all their time shut in her room, making this dreadful yowling sound. Sometimes it's so bad I have to take my football down to the park, just to get away from it all.

"You look a right idiot," I said.

"Mum!" yelled Izzie. "Did you hear what he said? Do something!"

"You look lovely, dear," said Mum. (I could tell she was lying.) "Haven't you got any homework, Josh?"

I muttered something.

"What?" said Izzie. "What did you say?"

"None of your business," I said.

"Josh!" said Mum. "You can tell me. What is it?"

"Oh – nothing!" I said. "We've got to write a poem. About an animal."

My sister scoffed.

"You can't do it, can you?" she said.

"Of course he can," said Mum. "You're both good at poetry."

"Correction!" said Izzie. "**I'm** good at poetry. I'm always writing songs for the band. It's dead easy."

"I've read you enough poetry, Josh," said Mum. "I'm sure you've got the idea by now."

She was right about one thing. She **had** read us enough poetry. Other children got Winnie-the-Pooh and Kipper stories at bedtime. We got the Lady of Shallot and Morte d'Arthur. Our Mum read us long, dismal poems that made your hair stand on end. If you didn't fall asleep first, that is.

"You remember 'The Rime of the Ancient Mariner', don't you?" said Mum.

Remember 'The Rime of the Ancient Mariner'! I should think so! It was all about an old bloke who

grabs someone on his way to a wedding. Then he bores him stiff, whining on and on about some boat-trip that went wrong. I had thought it was never going to end.

"There was an animal in that," said Mum. "Well, a bird, anyway. Can you remember what it was?"

My mind went blank.

"An ostrich?" I said.

Izzie bellowed with laughter.

"It was an albatross, dumbo!" she said.

I glared at her.

"That's what I meant," I said.

"I think you should just get on with it, Josh," said Mum and she frowned at Izzie. "Go on – try. I'm sure you can do it."

"Fat chance!" sniggered my sister as I went out

of the room; and she kicked my ankle, but secretly, so that Mum couldn't see.

It was that kick that did it. The more I think about it, I'm sure of it. If Izzie hadn't kicked me, I would never have seen the ghost.

# Chapter 2

I sat in my room, chewing a pencil, and tried to think of a poem. But really my mind was on Izzie. You'd think just being older than me would be enough for her, wouldn't you? But it's not. She always has to be top dog. She's louder than me. Cleverer than me. Bigger than me. (That's why I hadn't tried to kick her back; she always wins.)

"I'll show her!" I thought and chewed harder at my pencil. I chewed and I chewed but nothing came.

Our cat, Merlin, wandered into the room and rubbed himself against my leg.

"That's it!" I thought. "A cat! I'll write a poem

about a cat."

I wrote:

*"Once I had a little cat.*
*It got squashed flat.*
*Poor little cat."*

I sat and stared at my poem. I knew it wasn't quite right. Miss Wilson had said we had to write at least eight lines. This was only three.

Then I was struck by an idea. A really good idea, though I say it myself. I tip-toed along the landing and Merlin padded after me.

The walls of Mum's room were lined with shelves and most of them were packed with poetry books. I stood on the bed. I couldn't reach the highest shelf so I decided to do a bit of bouncing. One! Two! Three! I went higher and higher and on the last bounce I just managed to snatch a book.

I tip-toed back to my room and examined my catch. It was very dusty, for a start, which I thought was a good sign. Mum couldn't have looked at it for years – if ever. "Little-Known Victorian Verse," it said on the front.

Better still! I started flicking through the pages. If it was 'little-known' no-one would be able to tell if I'd written it or not, would they? I flicked on. Some of the poems were very long. Much too long for what I needed.

Hallo! Here was a shorter poem. "Alexander Twistleton-Tharpe; 1810-1895," it said at the top of the page. There was even a little drawing of him. He was a strange-looking, **long** man; everything about him was long – long beard, long hair and a long nose, with a pair of round, pebbly glasses balanced across it.

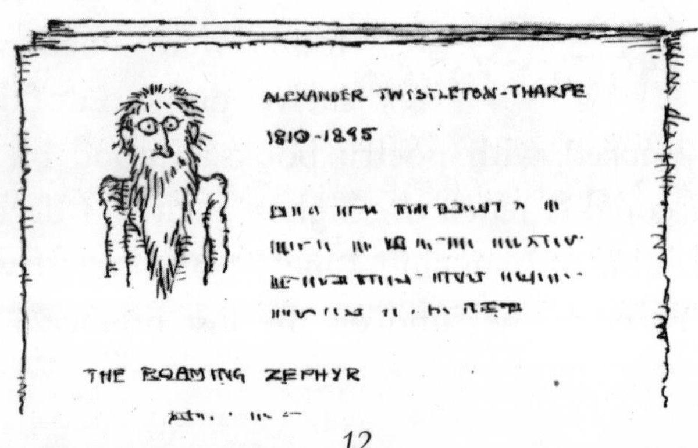

"Twistleton-Tharpe must have written thousands of poems in his long life," it said underneath. "We offer 'The Roaming Zephyr' as a taste of his work. Unfortunately, like his other poems, it has not stood the test of time."

Better and better! I read on. This is how it went:

*A roaming zephyr drifted o'er the Downs,*
*Threading the bosky slopes at break of day;*
*Rustling the sedges of the sullen mere,*
*It frolicked blithely on its jocund way.*

*It chased away the darkling shades of night,*
*Greeted the milkmaids and the shepherd lad.*
*It whispered in the blushing ear of dawn –*
*It touched the waiting world and made it glad.*

There were a lot of words here I'd never heard of. 'Bosky'? 'Sedges'? 'Jocund'? What did they mean? And who was this Dawn who was having her ear whispered into? I hadn't got a clue. Miss Wilson was going to guess something was up if I wasn't careful. I supposed I'd have to alter it a bit. I picked up my pencil. A zephyr? What was that? Probably an animal, a bit like a zebra. I started to write and went on writing. My poem was finished so quickly I surprised myself. This was it:–

The Lonely Zebra. By Josh Weller

*A lonely zebra wandered into town,*
*Trotting around the streets at break of day.*
*It busted through the hedges on the Rec*
*And messed about all down Jocasta Way.*

I had an idea that 'frolicked' meant 'messing about' and there was a road near us called Jocasta Way – that sounded quite like 'jocund', didn't it? My poem went on –

*It wore its shades and chased away the cats,*
*It scared the milkman and it kicked Kev's Dad.*
*It whinnied through the letter-box –*
*It woke me up, it did. And I felt glad.*

I sat back and read it over. Brilliant! I was a genius! I read it again. It was better than Twistleton-Tharpe's effort, anyway. At least you could understand what it was about. I tip-toed back to Mum's room and bounced the book back onto its shelf.

"That's one in the eye for you, Izzie!" I thought.

"Meeow!" said Merlin and he started to purr.

# Chapter 3

When I went downstairs Mum had her nose in a book and Izzie was shouting down the phone at one of her friends.

" 'Off-key?' " she bawled. "I'm never off-key. You've had it now, Samantha – you're out!"

Izzie was always throwing her friends out of the band.

"And another thing!" she bellowed. "You're way too fat for that crop-top!"

They'd have made up again by tomorrow. If I had been Samantha, I'd never have spoken to Izzie again. And I'd have had her boiled in oil, too.

"How's the homework going?" asked Mum,

glancing up.

"Oh – O.K." I said; and that was that.

I took my football into the back yard and had a good kick-about against the fence until Mr Jones, our next-door neighbour, leaned out of the bedroom window and yelled at me to stop.

That night I dreamed I was playing centre-forward for England and that I'd been made captain.

I also dreamed I was voted European Footballer of the Year. It was a really good dream; one of the best I've ever had.

. . . . . . . . . . . . .

I handed in my homework and forgot all about it. Until Thursday, that is.

Miss Wilson came in, looking flushed, and placed

her folder on her desk. She opened it and looked up.

"I was very pleased with your poetry homework," she said. "Most of you have tried very hard and made a really good job of it."

She looked straight at me and my heart sank into my trainers.

She'd sussed me! Somehow or other, she'd worked it out. Just my luck. I got ready with my excuses.

"But you, Josh," said Miss Wilson. "You –"

This was it! I braced myself.

"You," continued Miss Wilson, "You have really excelled yourself. Come up here."

I couldn't move. Strong roots were snaking downwards from the soles of my feet, down through the floor and down, down, down into the earth beneath ....

"Come on, Josh," repeated Miss Wilson.

I wrenched myself up and stumbled to the front of the class.

Thirty pairs of eyes stared at me in amazement.

"Josh has written a wonderful poem," said Miss Wilson. "It's called 'The Lonely Zebra.' I'm giving him a gold star for it."

The class looked even more amazed.

"And I'm going to ask him to read it to you," said Miss Wilson. "Over to you, Josh."

She handed me my poem. I stood and stared at it. I could feel my face growing hot. I tried to speak, but I found I'd been struck dumb.

"Josh?" said Miss Wilson encouragingly.

I just stood there.

"It's not always easy reading in front of an audience," said Miss Wilson. "Would you like me to read it for you?"

I made a sound like a hamster squeaking.

So Miss Wilson stood there and recited my poem while I went redder and redder. What a nightmare! I could hear some of my friends sniggering, especially when she got to the last line.

"It's a lovely poem!" said Miss Wilson. "You should feel very proud of yourself, Josh. It's quite funny, but it's very sad, too. How long did it take you?"

"Not very long," I mumbled, finding my voice.

"Class!" Miss Wilson's voice rang out, loud and clear, as I stumbled back to my seat. "We have a real poet amongst us!"

# Chapter 4

And that was the start of it.

My friends started calling me 'The Poet', or 'Lonely Zebra' or just plain 'Lonely'. Even some of the other classes got to hear about it.

" 'Ere, Zebra Boy!" yelled Dobber Dawson from the year above. "Come over 'ere and say us a poem, then!"

I looked the other way and kept walking. I could hear Dobber and his friends laughing like hyenas. It was not a pleasant sound.

Worse still, a small girl called Alicia, who fancied herself as a poet, started following me around.

"You and I are kindred spirits, Josh," she said.

"Will you come to tea? I could read you my poem about rainbows if you like."

No! I would definitely **not** like. I sprinted off as fast as I could. Alicia ran after me but she just wasn't quick enough. And it didn't end there. Miss Wilson got talking to my mother after school one day and the next thing I know Mum's boasting about me to all her friends. She's even run off dozens of photocopies of 'The Lonely Zebra' and she's handing them out to everyone she knows.

"Liked your poem!" said Mr Aziz at the corner shop. "Tell me – why exactly was the zebra lonely?"

"What are you working on at the moment, Josh?" called the postman through the letterbox.

"Mum!" I pleaded. "Can't you stop giving out those photocopies? Please! It's so embarrassing!"

"Oh, Josh, you are a funny old thing!" said my Mum. "Miss Wilson said you seemed very shy about your poem in class – that's so sweet!"

" 'Sweet' my foot!" snorted Izzie, looking like thunder.

That was the one good thing about all this – Izzie was really jealous. She couldn't bear to think I'd done well at something.

"I'm just so proud of you!" continued Mum. "I want everyone to read your poem – I always knew this family would produce a poet one day."

That night Mum read us a poem called 'The Forsaken Merman' before we went to bed. She kept looking at me as she was reading and at the end she said "What did you think of that, Josh?"

I'd been day-dreaming; I was just about to take

a free kick for England, so I was caught on the hop. Luckily, I have a reply that always goes down well at times like these.

"I liked the descriptions," I said.

Mum looked pleased and closed the book.

"Bedtime!" she said.

"You little weasel, Josh!" hissed my sister as we went upstairs. "Don't think for a minute you can get away with this! I bet you didn't write 'The Lonely Zebra' yourself. You didn't, did you?"

# Chapter 5

There was no way I was going to tell Izzie the truth. I did feel a bit bad about Mum and Miss Wilson; but they seemed so delighted with my poem it would have been a shame to spoil things for them.

And it was strange, but as time went on the more I came to believe I really had written 'The Lonely Zebra' myself. I found myself telling Mr Aziz that the zebra was lonely because it had run away from a zoo and was missing its friends; and I told the postman I was writing a new, very long poem about a whale.

At school the teasing died away and I became

a bit of a hero. I walked around with a swagger or sometimes I'd sit, just staring into space. The kids would nudge each other and whisper:

"Ssh! Don't disturb Josh – he's composing."

Then, just as everything was going really well for me, I was hit – Pow! – by a Big Disaster. And I really mean BIG.

"I have a special announcement to make," said Mr Noakes in Assembly one Monday morning. "Every year this school sends a few children to attend the Personal Development Course at Grimblethorpe Abbey. I'm going to read you a list of the children chosen to attend the dance, drama, football and athletics courses at Easter."

I held my breath as he started reeling off a list of names. "Please, please, **please** let me be on the football course!" I prayed.

It didn't work. I wasn't on the list – but my best friend Kevin was.

"Never mind, Josh," he whispered. "I'll teach you all the stuff I learn when I come back."

Mr Noakes was still speaking.

"And here's a surprise!" he said. "There's a new Poetry Category this year. Two children have been chosen – Alicia Sykes for her poem about the

rainbow and Josh Weller for his interesting poem called 'The Lonely Zebra.' We felt that both these children showed such promise they thoroughly deserved to go on the trip."

Kevin nudged me.

"Yeah, Josh! Great!" he said. "We're both going!"

I didn't answer. I felt as though a deep pit had opened beneath me. A pit full of spikes and snakes and crocodiles and I was falling ... falling ...

Aaargh! I'd hit the bottom. I was going on a poetry course. With Alicia Sykes.

"What's up, Josh?" asked Kevin as we filed back into class. "You look as though you've seen a ghost."

Miss Wilson overheard him.

"Just sit quietly for a moment, Josh," she said. "It's probably the excitement."

My mind was racing. It was only two weeks to the Easter holidays. How was I going to get myself out of this?

"It's such an opportunity, Josh," said Miss Wilson. "You'll be taught by a famous poet. You are a lucky boy – you'll learn all about scansion and similes and metaphors."

What were they? I really didn't want to know. I'd been looking forward to the holidays – kicking my football around, just hanging out. And now it looked as though I'd be back at school! Doing poetry. With Alicia Sykes. The last thing any boy in his right mind would want to do in the holidays.

And then another idea hit me. I'd be found out, wouldn't I? I could see the look on Mum's face. On Miss Wilson's face. I could hear the whole class sniggering. And worst of all, I could hear Izzie sneering –

"What did I say? I thought so all the time."

I knew I had to do something drastic.

# Chapter 6

I tried everything I knew. I really did. I pulled out all the stops. I kicked off with Plan Number One.

"Mum," I said as she was tucking me in one night. "I don't want to go away on this Personal Development Course. I want to stay here with you and Izzie."

"Yah!" said Izzie, sticking her head round the door. "What's up, Zebra Boy? Scared you'll be found out?"

"Ssh!" said Mum. "It's just nerves, Josh. You'll be fine when you get there. It's the chance of a lifetime – and it's only for a few days, after all."

She wouldn't budge so I had to put Plan Two

into operation. We were only a week away from countdown now.

"Mum," I said. "I've heard the kids get really badly treated at Grimblethorpe Abbey. You only get gruel to eat and they make you scrub the floors."

"It sounds a bit like 'Oliver!' " said my Mum brightly. "It should make a nice change – you never scrub the floors at home."

I could hear Izzie sniggering in the kitchen.

"I **heard**," I said, "that they came home one kid short last year. He was on the drama course. No-one ever saw him again. They think he fell down a well."

Mum put down her book and burst out laughing.

"Oh, you are funny, Josh!" she said. "You shouldn't believe everything you hear at school. That's just rubbish."

I was desperate; time was running out. And now here we were, with only three days to go, and I knew I'd have to put Plan Three into operation.

I painted spots all over my face with Izzie's lipstick and refused to get up that morning. Mum came in and peered at me and put a hand on my forehead.

"My tummy hurts, Mum!" I moaned.

Izzie appeared in the doorway, waving something in her hand. "Mum!" she yelled. "He's been at my lipstick! Look at it – it's ruined! Do something!"

Thank you, Izzie.

"Oh Josh," said my Mum, rubbing the spots off my face. "What are we going to do with you?"

"Send him on a Personal Development Course!" snapped Izzie. "Perhaps he'll develop from a monster into a boy."

"You **will** enjoy it, Josh," said Mum, ruffling my hair. "And you'd better get up or you'll be late for school."

. . . . . . . . . . . . .

And now it was Sunday night. My rucksack was packed. Mum had set the alarm. I lay in bed, staring into blackness. What was I going to do?

The door creaked and a horrible apparition hovered in mid-air. It was Izzie. She was holding a torch under her chin so she looked like a ghoul. She shone the torch at me, padded across the room and sat on my chest.

"Get off, Izzie!" I gasped.

It was like being pinned down by a two-ton elephant.

" 'Bella', you little ferret," said my sister. "Call me 'Bella'."

"Get off, Bella," I wheezed.

"Gruel?" whispered Izzie. "Scrubbing floors? Boys down wells?" She was holding the torch under her chin again. She looked really evil. "You know **nothing** about Grimblethorpe Abbey. Some of my friends went there last year."

"So?" I managed to gasp.

"And it's really, really scary," said Izzie. "There are strange noises at night and lights that move about. Monks lived there. They still have their tombs down in the crypt."

"Don't care!" I quavered.

"You **will** care!" said my sister. "You won't stand the pace – you'll be begging to come home. There's ghosts – ghosts of old dead monks, rattling

chains and carrying their heads under their arms. Be afraid, Josh. Be very, very afraid."

Then she was gone, as suddenly as she had come and the room was plunged into blackness.

I switched on the bedside light and lay staring at the ceiling. Monks! Ghosts! Tombs! Was it true? I didn't know whether to believe Izzie or not. At last I fell asleep and the next thing I knew it was morning and Mum was shaking me awake.

# Chapter 7

So here it was, D-Day. Doomsday. It had come at last. And the sun was shining away for all it was worth as though there was nothing wrong at all.

"Can I sit next to you, Josh?" asked Alicia as we piled into the school mini-bus; but I'd already had a word with Kevin and he plonked himself down next to me.

Alicia looked disappointed and sat next to Lydia Prescott, who was doing the drama course.

There were seven of us altogether – me, Kevin, Alicia, Lydia, Barney Woods, who was doing the football along with Kevin, and a long, skinny kid called Marvin, who was meant to be really good at high jump and was doing athletics. There was also someone called Edward who'd been put on the dance course.

Mr Poole was driving the mini-bus and Miss Wilson was coming with us, too. There was a rumour going round that they were in love, so as the mini-bus revved up we started whispering jokes about them holding hands and kissing until Mr Poole said, "That's enough of that! Settle down!"

So we started teasing Edward instead.

"Brought your tights, Edward?" asked Kevin and everyone laughed.

Edward was small and pale. He just sat there without saying a word.

"I'm not telling you again!" said Mr Poole as he steered the mini-bus onto the motorway.

We bowled along in the inside lane, singing songs

and telling jokes and after a while I began to feel almost happy – at least, I stopped being miserable. I forgot about my poem and I forgot about the ghosts.

After half an hour or so we came off the motorway and drove through a little town; and Mr Poole swung the mini-bus between two enormous gate-posts with stone pineapples on top.

"Look, children!" said Miss Wilson. "There's Grimblethorpe Abbey!"

Far below us we could see a cluster of dark spires poking up above the trees.

We drew closer and we could see that the front of the building was covered in carvings – there were lots of saintly-looking guys with beards and long dresses; they held books and crosses and doves and looked skywards with fed-up expressions on their faces. Ugly heads leaned from the guttering; they pulled disgusting faces, as though someone had put a school dinner in front of them.

"Gargoyles," said Mr Poole.

"What are those things flying round the roof?" asked Kevin.

"Vampire bats!" said Marvin.

"Don't be silly, Marvin," said Miss Wilson. "They're pigeons."

The mini-bus scrunched to a halt on the gravel forecourt. We seized our rucksacks and joined the kids from other schools who were also climbing out of their buses.

"This way!" said Miss Wilson and we followed her through the front door and into the entrance hall. It was rather dark and gloomy; the only light came from stained glass windows that threw splashes of red and blue and violet across the floor and over the rows of statues that stood in alcoves along the wall.

"Oo-er!" said Kevin, clutching my arm.

Though there was no draught, the tattered

banners that hung from the ceiling were moving gently up and down.

"Ghosts!" said Barney. "There's ghosts here! Everybody says so."

# Chapter 8

"I think I'm going to like Grimblethorpe Abbey," said Kevin. "It's really cool."

We'd had a brilliant lunch in the Refectory - pizza, chips and chocolate gateau - and after that we'd been taken on a tour of the Abbey. Now we were lying around on our beds in the dormitory.

"**Two** football pitches! And a rugby pitch!" I said.

"And what about the high-jump pit?" said Marvin. "And the running-track? Those kids are really lucky."

Grimblethorpe Abbey had stopped being an abbey years ago and was a boarding-school. In the holidays they rented it out for courses like the one we were on.

"The best bit's the crypt!" chimed in Tim, a boy from another school. "All those tombs! Is that creepy or what?"

I didn't say anything. The crypt was below the chapel and was strictly off-limits; but they'd let us take a peep as we'd filed past the entrance. It was dark and musty and made me shiver; and I'd suddenly thought of Izzie.

Mr Poole and another teacher popped their heads round the door.

"Don't forget, everyone," said Mr Poole. "Meeting this evening in the Great Hall. Don't be late! You're going to be introduced to your course tutors."

"Sir!" shouted Barney. "Is it true that Wayne Boxall's going to take us for football?"

Wayne Boxall was the captain of Barchester United. They said there was a good chance of him being picked for England next time. I had a big signed poster of him on my bedroom wall.

Mr Poole and the other teacher grinned.

"Wait and see!" said Mr Poole.

After they'd gone the footballers in the room went mad. They started making 'Yip-yip-yip' sounds and jumping around on their beds. Kevin joined them.

I lay there feeling dead jealous. What wouldn't I give to be on a course with Wayne Boxall! And instead of that I was having to study poetry. **Poetry!** I decided life wasn't fair. No! It wasn't fair at all.

# Chapter 9

So here we were, in the Great Hall, listening to Mrs Court, who was in charge of the Personal Development Course. I looked around as Mrs Court rabbited on into the mike. What a place! There were chandeliers hanging from the ceilings and they sparkled on the panelled walls and the floors and the red curtains that framed the stage.

Mrs Court was coming to the end of her speech.

"And now!" she cried. "The moment you've all been waiting for – the course tutors!"

She nodded towards the side of the stage, where the tutors were sitting, half-hidden in the shadows.

"First of all," she said, "the football tutor. I'm sure he needs no introduction – Mr Wayne Boxall!"

Everyone went mad. The kids were on their feet, whistling and stamping and some of the girls were making little screaming noises.

Wayne Boxall sauntered to the middle of the stage. He was wearing a pair of long shorts that ended about six inches above his ankles and his hair was gelled into a pink spike. He wore a diamond ring in his nose and it sparkled in the light.

"Hi, kids!" he said, leaning towards the mike and keeping his hands in his pockets. "Cool!"

And that was about it. He sauntered back to his seat and the screaming died down. Mrs Court went on to introduce the tutors for drama, athletics and dance. They all had a bit more to say for themselves than Wayne Boxall. The dance tutor even did a little tap-dance.

Mrs Court was speaking again.

"And last of all," she was saying, "Our poetry tutor – "

I looked up glumly. I supposed he or she would be a right dork. A tall figure rose to its feet and loped towards the mike. Hang on! He looked familiar! Hadn't I seen him before somewhere?

"– our poetry tutor, Alexander Twistleton-Tharpe," said Mrs Court.

What? My head jerked back in horror. I felt as though someone had stuck a red-hot needle in me. Of course I'd seen him before! That face – it was the very one that had stared out at me from "Little-Known Victorian Verse!" It was the author of "The Roaming Zephyr!" And what was worse, he seemed to be

looking straight at me.

I panicked. I had to get out of here. I got up and started pushing my way along the row. Twistleton-Tharpe had begun to speak, but I didn't hear a word of it.

I groped my way through the door and out into the corridor. I leaned against the wall. I'd been found out! But it couldn't really be Twistleton-Tharpe, could it? He'd been dead for over a century.

If not, he had to be about two hundred years old by now.

There could only be one explanation. I'd cheated and I'd been found out. And now Twistleton-Tharpe's ghost had come back to haunt me. What was I going to do?

"Josh!" It was Miss Wilson's voice. She must have followed me out of the hall. "Whatever's the matter? You're shaking like a leaf!"

# Chapter 10

"I feel sick!" I gasped. It was the truth; I really did.

Miss Wilson looked at me, her head on one side.

"It may have something to do with all that chocolate gateau you ate at lunch," she said. "And you probably overdid the cakes at tea-time, too."

I stared at her. I could feel my mouth hanging open. Exactly how unsympathetic could you get?

"The best thing you can do," continued Miss Wilson, "is to have an early night. You'll feel better in the morning."

I nodded dumbly and turned away.

"And don't forget!" Miss Wilson called after me. "Your first workshop's at a quarter to ten tomorrow morning. You're in Room Seventeen."

My heart was thumping nineteen to the dozen. The same thought kept going round and round in my head. What was I going to do? I was trapped – walled up in Grimblethorpe Abbey with a ghost! A ghost who was obviously out to get me.

I was already panicking like mad when I heard the rattling sound. It was coming slowly towards me down the dimly-lit corridors. Oh no! It must be that headless monk Izzie had mentioned. The rattling drew nearer.

Or perhaps it was Twistleton-Tharpe, roaming the Abbey, looking for the boy who had stolen his poem. The rattling drew closer and closer. Whatever it was was about to appear round the corner.

I stood still, frozen to the spot with horror.

. . . . . . . . . . . . .

"Night-night, sonny!" said the tea-lady as she bustled past me with her trolley.

I stood, still frozen to the spot, as the sound of rattling cups faded away into the distance. Gradually my pulse returned to normal. I raced up to the dormitory and dived into bed.

I lay there, trembling, whilst outside the owls hooted and, for all I knew, the ghost of Twistleton-Tharpe drifted around the spires and peered through the windows. I pulled the covers over my head; I hardly dared to breathe. I don't know how long I lay there, but I must have dropped off at last; because the next thing I knew it was morning.

# Chapter 11

I was woken by the sound of muffled voices. People were moving about and I could hear the occasional 'Snip-snip' of scissors.

I kept my eyes tight shut but my mind was racing round and round in circles, like a dog chasing its tail. What was I going to do? Should I phone Mum and ask to come home? I could already see the smirk on Izzie's face as she said, "What did I tell you?"

No. That one was definitely a non-starter.

"Josh!"

Someone was tugging at my duvet. I peered out and saw Kevin. He'd gelled his hair into a pink cone and cut about six inches off the bottom of his track-suit trousers.

"Josh!" he repeated. "Have you got a diamond ring on you?"

"Of course I haven't," I said. "What do you want it for, anyway?"

"I want to wear it in my nose like Wayne Boxall," he said.

Yuk!

"I thought I could stick it on with Blu Tack," Kevin continued. "Are you **sure** you haven't got one?"

There was a lot of giggling coming from the doorway. The footballers had gathered there, ready for their early morning start; they were milling

around a big, mouthy kid called Rob Riley, who seemed to be their leader. And guess what? They **all** looked like Wayne Boxall, with pink cones on their heads and cut-down track-suits. Some of them had even managed to fix rings in their noses.

I groaned and dived back under the duvet where I lay listening to the footballers stampeding away into the distance.

"Everyone up!"

It was Mr Poole.

All around me the others started to stir and went off to breakfast, but I didn't budge; I just wasn't hungry.

"Josh!"

It was a girl's voice this time. Alicia Sykes shoved her head round the door.

"Don't be late for the poetry workshop!" she called. "We're going to read our poems out to Mr Twistleton-Tharpe. Isn't it exciting?"

"Go away!" I groaned. "I'm ill."

But Alicia had given me an idea. Miss Wilson

sometimes got us to read out our homework when she hadn't had time to read it herself. Perhaps Twistleton-Tharpe did this, too – it sounded like it, didn't it?

I looked at my watch. Nine-thirty. I had plenty of time – what had Miss Wilson said? A quarter past ten? If I went to Room Seventeen – now – I might be able to find my copy of 'The Lonely Zebra' and remove it before Twistleton-Tharpe had a chance to read it.

I flung on my clothes and raced off down the corridor. As I passed the big window at the top of the stairs I noticed the footballers doing star-jumps on the playing-field. Wayne Boxall jumped

up and down in front of them. He was wearing full-length trousers and his hair was blue and wavy.

I found Room Seventeen easily enough. The door was open and I peeped in. It was a big, musty room with cupboards running the length of one wall. There was a semi-circle of chairs, arranged in front of the desk, and on the desk – yes! – a pile of paperwork.

I tip-toed over and took a peek. It was our poems, right enough. I rifled through the pile and there, at the bottom, was 'The Lonely Zebra.' I grabbed it and got ready to go. It was then that I heard the footsteps in the corridor – and, worst of all, the voice of Twistleton-Tharpe.

"Good – you're all on time," he was saying. "This way – I've got the room ready for you."

. . . . . . . . . . . . .

Help! I looked around wildly. I must have got the time wrong! The footsteps and the voices came nearer and nearer and I heard the door-handle turn. There was only one thing for it. I jumped into a cupboard and closed the door behind me. I cowered there in the dark, clutching 'The Lonely Zebra' to my chest.

Not a moment too soon! I heard people coming into the room and the scrape of chairs. I peered through the key-hole. I could see Twistleton-Tharpe standing at his desk, stroking his long beard. I half-expected him to remove his head and place it

under his arm, or to drift off through the wall behind him. But neither of these things happened.

"Welcome, everyone!" said Twistleton-Tharpe. "I hope this is going to be a pleasant experience for us all."

Oh yes? Being taught by a ghost? Just how pleasant was that going to be?

I heard the rustling of paper.

"Here are the poems your teachers sent in," said Twistleton-Tharpe. "I'm going to ask you to read them out."

Phew! I breathed a sigh of relief.

Twistleton-Tharpe went on calling out people's names and handing out poems. He came to the end and I was congratulating myself on a successful operation when –

"Hallo!" said Twistleton-Tharpe. "Where's Josh Weller?"

I held my breath.

"He's not well, sir!" piped up Alicia. "He's in bed."

"That's a pity," said Twistleton-Tharpe. "I was looking forward to meeting our Mr Weller."

Was it my imagination, or was there a hint of menace in his voice?

"And his poem's not here, either," said Twistleton-Tharpe. "That's strange. Oh well – it doesn't matter. I've got it down on disk – I'll do a print-out later."

Foiled! Just my luck. Twistleton-Tharpe, a Victorian ghost, had caught up with new technology! Who'd have thought it? I sank to the floor in despair.

I realised that I was sitting on something

uncomfortable, like the bristles of a large scrubbing-brush, but I couldn't move. And there I had to stay while Alicia read her poem.

"Oh, pretty rainbow in the sky –" she began; and almost immediately I dozed off, in spite of the excruciating pain in my backside. I was only woken by the scraping of chairs.

"See you all this afternoon," said Twistleton-Tharpe. "Good luck with the project – just try to enjoy it."

"Oh, thank you, sir, we will!" said Alicia in a drippy voice.

"Oh – and if anyone sees Josh Weller," said Twistleton-Tharpe as the room emptied, "send him along to see me, will you? There's something I need to discuss with him – urgently."

. . . . . . . . . . . . .

I made sure the coast was clear, then I made a bee-line for the dormitory. When I got there I stuffed 'The Lonely Zebra' into the back of my locker. Then I dived into bed and pulled the duvet over my head.

# Chapter 12

"Josh Weller!" It was Mr Poole's voice. "What are you doing in bed?"

"I'm ill, sir," I faltered. I'd been hiding there for over an hour.

"Hmm!" said Mr Poole. He tapped my feet, which must have been sticking out of the bottom of the duvet. "And do you usually go to bed with your trainers on?"

I'd been rumbled. I sat up, blinking, and saw Miss Wilson standing there, too.

"You've got **all** your clothes on, Josh," she said reproachfully.

"Open your mouth and say 'Aah' ", said

Mr Poole.

"Aah!" I said.

"Now stick out your tongue," he commanded.

They both leaned forward.

"It looks perfectly healthy to me," said Miss Wilson. "Any spots? Rashes?"

"No," I muttered.

"I think you're shamming," said Mr Poole.

"Mr Twistleton-Tharpe tells me you missed his workshop," said Miss Wilson. "I know you're shy about your poetry, Josh, but this just won't do. Come down and have some lunch – that'll make you feel better."

"Then you can join the other poets in the rose-garden," added Mr Poole. "They're having a brain-storming session."

They led me down to the Refectory. Most people had finished but the dinner-ladies managed to

find me some shepherd's pie, followed by the most ginormous helping of apple tart and custard I'd ever seen in my life.

I was ready for it, I can tell you. As I finished the last spoonful, I heard giggling and there, half-concealed behind a pillar, were Miss Wilson and Mr Poole.

"Nothing much wrong with him, then," Miss Wilson was saying.

"I think he'll survive," said Mr Poole.

And with that they marched forwards and hauled me off into the open air.

It was all happening. The sound of music and the thumping of feet floated from the Dance Studio and under some trees in the distance I could see the drama group doing something dramatic. The footballers were on the pitch and the athletes were running round and round the track; Marvin was leaping about in the high-jump pit, looking like a skinny stick-insect.

The poets were sitting round a fountain.

"Are you feeling better, Josh?" asked Alicia, making room for me next to her.

I said nothing but I sat down. Mr Poole and Miss Wilson nodded approvingly and moved away.

"We're brainstorming on 'Water' " said Alicia.

"We have to talk about all the things water reminds us of and then write them down. Shall I start, everyone?"

And they were off.

"Rainbows dancing in the spray," said Alicia in her drippy voice.

"Ripples," said another kid.

"Clouds reflecting," said someone else.

At last it was my turn and, as usual, my mind went blank. Suddenly, something came rising up from the depths of my memory – so suddenly it took me by surprise. It was like a giant squid surfacing.

"Water, water, everywhere – nor any drop to drink," I said.

They all looked at me in astonishment.

"That's lovely, Josh," said Alicia. "You are clever."

Oh no! I was at it again! I'd pinched it from 'The Rime of the Ancient Mariner'.

As if on cue, Twistleton-Tharpe appeared. He came strolling over the lawn with his hands behind

his back and his nose in the air. It was as though he'd been conjured up by an evil spirit. I watched carefully in case he drifted through the clipped box trees and the rose arches, but nothing like that happened; he just came steadily towards us with his long, loping stride.

"I'm out of here," I muttered; and I raced off, bending low behind a box hedge. I found myself on the touchline of the football pitch, so I ran on and mingled with the players. I hoped no-one would notice, and for a while, no-one did.

I looked back at the poets. Twistleton-Tharpe had joined them and was stooping down, examining their notes.

"Josh!" hissed Kevin. "What are you doing?"

I passed the ball back to him and was about to answer when –

"Sir!" It was Rob Riley. I'd had a feeling

he hadn't liked me from the start. "There's a poet here! That's not fair, sir! They've got one more than us!"

"You! Off!" yelled Wayne Boxall, pointing.

I sloped off the field and skulked around until I was sure Twistleton-Tharpe had disappeared again. Then I rejoined the poets. They were brainstorming over something else now.

"Where have you been, Josh?" cried Alicia; and without waiting for an answer she said, "We've got to think of scary things. Spiders! Ooh! All hairy and sticky! I hate them!"

It went round the circle. Everyone had something to say.

"Skeletons!"

"Vampire bats, flying round your house at night!"

"Werewolves howling in the woods!"

It came to my turn and I hesitated.

"Ghosts!" I said at last. "Ghosts who are coming to get you!"

# Chapter 13

"I've been down the crypt!"

It was Rob Riley. We all turned and stared at him.

"Cor! Rob! You haven't, have you?" said Barney.

"I have!" said Rob. "And I can prove it. I've left my football scarf down there on a tomb."

The footballers crowded round him. They'd washed the pink cones from their hair and had been experimenting with powdered chalk.

Rob Riley looked like an Ancient Briton. The chalk dust had drifted down from his head and turned his face blue, so it seemed as though he was covered in woad.

I was feeling relaxed; admitting I was scared of ghosts had calmed me down. I'd just decided that Twistleton-Tharpe was human after all. Whether it was the relief or whether it was the sight of Rob with his blue face, I don't know; but I just couldn't help myself. I burst out laughing.

Rob rounded on me.

"What's so funny, you little squirt?" he demanded.

"Nothing," I said.

Rob pushed me in the chest.

"Dear little poet!" he scoffed. "Does he want to play football with the big boys, then?"

Kevin looked worried but he didn't say anything.

At that moment Edward came into the room. He was carrying the bag that held his dance things. Rob immediately lost interest in me, probably because he'd found someone even smaller to pick on.

"Hallo! It's our ickle ballerina!" he sneered.

Some of the footballers sniggered.

Edward didn't say anything. He always kept himself to himself, anyway. He just glanced at Rob with his huge eyes and started to pack his things away into his locker.

"Go on – show us your tutu!" jeered Rob.

Edward still didn't say anything. This seemed to drive Rob mad. He advanced on Edward and started pushing him about. The others didn't do anything to stop him.

He grabbed Edward's bag and scattered its contents over the floor. There were shorts, tap-shoes, footless tights and a book called 'Swan Lake'.

"You're a wimp!" said Rob.

"I'm not!" said Edward suddenly. It was the first time any of us had heard him speak. "You have to be really strong to lift ballerinas in the air."

Rob fell about laughing.

Then he stopped and shoved his face into Edward's.

"Little dancing boy!" he said. "I bet you're a coward – too scared to do anything much, aren't you?"

"I'm not!" said Edward; he'd fallen into Rob's trap.

"In that case," said Edward, grinning from ear to ear, "You prove it."

"Alright – I will," said Edward.

A hush fell on the room. Everyone except Edward had guessed what Rob was going to say.

Rob spoke very slowly and softly.

"O.K.", he said. "Then you go down to the crypt – tonight – and get my scarf for me. I've left it on the big tomb at the far end."

Edward turned white. I could see him struggling for words.

And suddenly I could bear it no longer. I looked at Rob, towering above Edward with his big, blue face, and all at once I realised who he reminded me of. It was Izzie. And I remembered how I never – ever – stood up to her.

"Just you lay off him, Rob!" I shouted.

"O.K. – I will," sneered Rob. "But only if you go instead, poet."

"It's a deal!" I said.

Kevin clutched at my arm.

"Josh – no!" he hissed.

Rob laughed.

"That's right – you listen to your friend," he scoffed. "You won't even get as far as the cloisters. You haven't got the bottle."

That did it!

"Oh no?" I said. "Just you watch me!"

# Chapter 14

So here I was, late at night, creeping along the cloisters. Frost shimmered on the lawn and the owls were hooting in the woods. Kev had lent me his torch and I clutched it tightly in my right hand.

I was so angry I was all fired up. I didn't feel scared. But as I approached the door of the crypt I realised that Rob had had two advantages over me. One: he'd been down to the crypt in daylight. And Two: the door had been open. Now it was the middle of the night – and to my dismay I found the door was chained up. I pushed at it. Though the chain held, the door itself wasn't fastened. It creaked open just a crack – just enough to let a small person through.

I hesitated. I was beginning to feel a bit worried. Then I thought of Izzie; and I thought of Rob, with his blue face, pushing Edward around. I drew a deep breath. I'd run straight in, snatch the scarf and run straight out again. This was it. I took another deep breath and wriggled through the gap. I scrabbled around for the light switch. I found it and flicked it up and down. Oh no! The lights weren't working. I'd have to rely on my torch. I edged my way down a flight of steps and paused at the bottom. The air smelled damp and musty. I flashed my torch the length of the crypt. There was a double row of pillars down the middle and tombs

everywhere. I started to run, still shining my torch and shadows leaped around the walls and ceiling like threatening giants.

At the far end of the crypt was a huge, raised

tomb with a sleeping stone figure on top. And there, sure enough, draped around the statue's neck, was a scarf.

I ran even faster, and my footsteps echoed like thunder around the vaulted roof. I reached the tomb, stretched up and snatched the scarf. My heart was pounding in my chest. I hadn't taken a breath since I'd entered the crypt. Now I did. I turned, ready to run again and the sweeping beam of my torch fell across a tombstone at the side of the aisle. A carved word leaped out at me. It grabbed me by the throat and held me fast. I stared and stared. "Twistleton," I read. "Twistleton-Tharpe. Poet. 1810 – 1895."

I felt as though a knife had gone through me. I couldn't move. I was still trying to force my legs forward when I became aware of a creaking sound somewhere behind the headstone. What was it? Rats? Bats? I couldn't tell.

It all happened so suddenly that afterwards it seemed like a bad dream. The creaking grew louder and I pointed my torch – and there, caught for a moment in its beam, and hovering above his own headstone, was the face of Twistleton-Tharpe! The torchlight glinted on his glasses.

I was unfrozen as if by magic. I didn't hang around, either.

I let out a shriek and bolted for the door. I lost my footing on the steps, scrambling and clawing up them in my panic; at any moment I expected to feel a cold hand on my shoulder. I reached the door and wriggled through.

And then I ran like mad.

. . . . . . . . . . . . .

The others sat up in bed as I burst into the dormitory. I must have looked as white as a sheet.

"Cor!" said Barney.

"What is it, Josh?" said Kevin. "What's happened?"

I couldn't speak. I rammed the scarf into Rob's hand and dived onto my bed. The others crowded round, asking questions and gazing at me in admiration, but I was speechless. I just lay there, staring into space. I hardly heard their voices.

All I could see was the strange, long face of Twistleton-Tharpe, floating in mid-air above his tombstone, his glasses flashing in the light of my torch.

# Chapter 15

I didn't sleep much that night and when I did nod off I dreamed of ghouls and bats and headless horsemen.

I was woken by the footballers. They trailed off to the Refectory, leaving patches of blue behind them on their pillows. Somehow or other I didn't fancy lying all alone with my thoughts; so I sprang up and ran after them.

"Kev!" I whispered as I caught up with him in the corridor. "Do you believe in ghosts?"

"Why? Did you see one?" asked Kevin. "Is that what happened last night?"

"Just answer my question," I said. "Do you?"

"No," said Kevin. He paused for a moment. "Not in the daytime, anyhow."

I sat there in the Refectory, surrounded by the clink of plates and cups and the hissing of the tea-urn. I could hear whispers passing round the room. Every so often I'd catch the odd word – "Ghost" … "Josh" … "Crypt" ….

I was feeling so bad I hardly took any notice.

"Five minutes!" called Wayne Boxall, appearing in the doorway.

The footballers groaned. Wayne Boxall was wearing baggy shorts over a pair of tights; he'd shaved his head completely and when he bent down to tie a shoe-lace everyone noticed that he'd a large football tattooed on his head.

"Got to go!" said Kev and the footballers were off, leaving a cloud of blue dust behind them. More people came into the room – the athletes and the dancers and after them the drama students and the poets. Still the whispers went on – "Josh Weller" … "Skeletons" … "Headless monks" …

I sat there silently, sunk in misery. And I would have sat there forever had not a cold hand suddenly descended on my shoulder.

"Josh Weller!" said a voice. "I want you at my workshop!"

. . . . . . . . . . . . .

I almost jumped out of my skin. There stood Alexander Twistleton-Tharpe, wearing a check shirt and a pair of long, khaki shorts.

I made a squeaking sound. Then he was gone, as silently as he'd arrived. I think I'd have stayed there forever; I couldn't move. But at twenty-to-ten sharp, Miss Wilson and Mr Poole appeared on either side of me, and, without saying a word, they took an arm each and marched me off to Room Seventeen.

The rest of the poets were already there.

"Aha! Josh Weller!" said Twistleton-Tharpe, his glasses glinting. "Nice of you to join us."

I took a seat as the group launched into a discussion on yesterday's brain-storming. There was a lot of laughter and people started to talk about their ideas. I hardly took anything in. I stared at Twistleton-Tharpe. All I saw was the dark crypt and that ghostly face hovering in mid-air.

Alicia was reading out the group's ideas about water.

"And this is what Josh thought of," she was saying. " 'Water, water, everywhere, Nor any drop to drink.' "

"Ah!" said Twistleton-Tharpe. "So you're acquainted with 'The Rime of the Ancient Mariner', Josh?"

Caught! I decided the thing to do was to keep quiet. I said nothing.

"It's a good poem, isn't it?" said Twistleton-Tharpe.

"Sir!" said Alicia. She sounded disappointed. "Do you mean Josh didn't write it himself?"

"No, but that's alright," said Twistleton-Tharpe.

"I asked you to talk about what came into your heads when you thought of water. It reminded Josh of a poem he'd read – I'm impressed."

He looked at me encouragingly, but I still didn't speak.

"Never mind!" he said. "Let's move on to the Scary project."

There was a lot more laughing and then people began to talk about how they could turn their ideas into poems.

"Josh!" said Twistleton-Tharpe. "You haven't said a word yet. I see from these notes that you're scared of ghosts." He looked me straight in the eye.

"Would you like to talk about ghosts? What sort of ghosts scare you? Why?"

I said nothing.

Of course, Alicia had to butt in.

"Josh has seen a ghost, sir!" she said.

"No – it was a vampire!" said another kid.

"It bit him on the neck!" said yet another.

"Hmm!" said Twistleton-Tharpe. "Haven't you anything at all to say, Josh?"

I pressed my lips together.

"Oh well," said Twistleton-Tharpe and he started reading the group some of his own poems. They must have been a lot funnier than 'The Roaming Zephyr' because everyone was soon in fits of laughter. I didn't take in a word; my thoughts were far away in the crypt.

I came to as people began to get to their feet.

"Just start composing your poems," Twistleton-Tharpe was saying. "And I'll come round this afternoon and check how you're getting on.

Tomorrow's the last full day and you'll be performing your poems in the Hall."

The last day! Thank goodness for that! I started for the door.

"Not so fast, Josh Weller," said Twistleton-Tharpe. "I want a word with you – it's about 'The Lonely Zebra'."

I didn't reply. I just lowered my head and ran for it.

# Chapter 16

I sat on a bench against the wall, trying to eat a cheese sandwich and keeping one eye open for Twistleton-Tharpe. I reckoned that if I kept my head down I'd get away with it; but I had to stay alert.

Kids kept coming up to me. I was famous now. The news about me standing up to Rob Riley had spread and, of course, they all tried to get me to talk about what I'd seen in the crypt. It was strange, being a bit of a hero and at the same time being half-scared to death – I could feel my insides going round like a washing machine. I wished, over and over again, that I'd never set eyes on 'Lesser-

Known Victorian Verse.'

"Josh Weller!"

Mr Poole strode towards me with blazing eyes and towered over me like an avenging angel.

"I've just been talking to Mr Twistleton-Tharpe!" he said. "He's asked me if you're an Electric Newt!"

I gaped at him. What was he talking about? And what was an electric newt? Some new kind of toy? A robot? A reptile? And why did Twistleton-Tharpe think I was one? It must be a trick to catch me out.

"What's an electric newt, sir?" I stammered.

"An elective mute, Cloth-ears!" roared Mr Poole.

"Someone who chooses not to speak."

"Oh," I said.

" 'Oh'?" repeated Mr Poole. " 'Oh?' Is that all you've got to say? I told Mr Twistleton-Tharpe that you're the biggest chatter-box in the school. You've been wasting his time."

"Sorry, sir," I muttered.

"Don't apologize to me," thundered Mr Poole. "You go and apologize to Mr Twistleton-Tharpe. **Now!** He's sitting by the fountain."

I slunk off. I glanced back at Mr Poole. I'd never seen him so cross. He was still standing there, arms folded.

Even though I was scared of Mr Poole, I was a million times more scared of Twistleton-Tharpe. So once I was out of sight I headed in the opposite direction to the fountain.

. . . . . . . . . . . . .

I found myself standing at the entrance to the Yew Tree Maze. I was happy with mazes. I'd once been to the Hampton Court Maze and Mum had told me how to find your way in and out again. So I thought the Grimblethorpe maze would be a piece of cake.

I set off, trailing my hand along the hedge, the way Mum had shown me. The trees grew quite thickly and soon the sound of people shouting on the playing fields died away. I was in a world of my own. No-one ever came here. I could spend the rest of the day in the maze and no-one would find me.

I rounded a corner. I'd come the right way, sure enough. A short alley led to the middle of the maze. I heard the gurgle of water and saw a fountain; the sunlight made rainbows in the spray. And there, sitting on a bench next to the fountain, his long nose buried in a book, was an all-too familiar figure.

He looked up and saw me and put down his book.

"Hallo, Josh!" said Alexander Twistleton-Tharpe. "I've been waiting for you."

# Chapter 17

"Aargh!" I gave a scream and turned tail.

"Josh!" yelled Twistleton-Tharpe and I could hear him coming after me.

I was in a total panic. I forgot all about following the hedges with my hand on the way back. I was so scared I even forgot which was my right hand and which was my left. I turned a corner and found myself facing a dead end.

Twistleton-Tharpe appeared behind me.

Fear gave me strength. I plunged into the yew-tree hedge on my right and forced my way through. I was soon covered in twigs and dusty black stuff and my nostrils were full of that yewy disinfectant smell, but I hardly noticed. I only knew I had to keep moving. I threw myself through hedge after hedge. And there, at last, was the entrance. I gasped with relief. Then I ran for all I was worth.

Behind me I could hear Twistleton-Tharpe shouting, "Josh! Come back!" but I just kept running. I rounded the corner of the Abbey and ran through the rose-garden, past the fountain where Twistleton-Tharpe was meant to be sitting. I raced across both the football pitches and after that the rugby pitch; I slowed down and glanced behind me. Oh no! Twistleton-Tharpe was still there! He galloped along in his khaki shorts, his skinny legs

working like pistons. Help! A lot of kids noticed what was happening and they started to shout.

"Come on, Josh! You're winning!"

"Go, Josh! Go!"

Was it my imagination, or was Twistleton-Tharpe gaining on me? I saw the woods a little way ahead and ran even faster. I plunged in amongst the trees and kept running. It was really creepy in there. I pounded past decaying, gnarled oak trees that must have been hundreds of years old; their branches snaked downwards like clutching arms. I could hear rabbits scarpering in the undergrowth.

I must have given him the slip by now! I paused, panting, and leaned against a tree. To my horror I heard the sound of thundering feet – and it was a sound that was drawing nearer and nearer. Round a bend in the path came Twistleton-Tharpe, loping along like the Last Of the Mohicans.

"Wait, Josh!" he yelled but I was off again.

I reached the other side of the wood and ran down a slope towards a lake. A crowd of geese and ducks kicked up a racket when they saw me coming and dived into the water, but I just kept going. I ran round the lake.

Once I'd reached the other side I looked across – and there was Twistleton-Tharpe, galloping along past the reed-beds. I couldn't believe it.

I started up a steep hill to my right. It slowed me down, and Twistleton-Tharpe began to gain on me. I was puffing and blowing now and I had a stitch – a bad one. I felt as though I'd got a huge dinner-plate stuck under my ribs. I forced myself upwards and reached the top of the hill.

I found myself on a narrow path, bordered by a hawthorn hedge. I took a right turn and kept running and after a while the stitch disappeared. I went faster. Surely I'd shaken him off?

I must have done.

"Josh!"

No such luck! There was nothing for it but to keep going. I soon realised I'd run myself into a corner. The path petered out and the way ahead was barred by a thick hedge and a barbed-wire fence; there was another hedge to my right. I looked wildly from side to side; I could hear Twistleton-Tharpe getting closer all the time.

To my left was a tree, almost completely smothered in ivy. It was my only chance. I scrambled up, seeking desperately for footholds, and wriggled

backwards along a branch. I lay as low as I could and burrowed down into the ivy.

I heard the pounding feet drawing nearer. Now they were slowing down; and now they were stopping – right beneath my tree. I forgot to breathe. And then, in the silence, the bough I was lying on gave a loud creak.

I looked down and almost lost my grip. I was hanging, hundreds of feet up, over an enormous drop!

# Chapter 18

"Josh! Josh! Are you up there?" called Twistleton-Tharpe.

I kept quiet. The branch gave another creak – louder this time.

"I know you're there!" called Twistleton-Tharpe. "Just come down – now – and everything will be alright."

What sort of an idiot did he think I was? I wasn't going to budge, you can bet your life. So here I was, caught between an angry ghost and a Big Drop. I looked down and saw the dark rocks below me like sharp, jutting teeth and the great yawning mouth of the quarry ready to swallow me up. I couldn't move.

The branch gave a louder creak, but this time it was more of a cracking sound. I hung on harder than ever as I felt the branch sag beneath me.

"That's it!" yelled Twistleton-Tharpe. "I'm coming up!"

I heard him rustling through the ivy. My branch sagged even lower and a jagged white split appeared in front of me. Then – horror of horrors – Twistleton-Tharpe's face appeared amongst the leaves. He was only a few feet away.

"Keep off!" I shouted.

Twistleton-Tharpe stopped moving.

"Why are you so scared of me?" he asked in a puzzled voice.

"You're a ghost!" I screamed. "Keep off!"

"A ghost?" repeated Twistleton-Tharpe. He

really sounded as though it was news to him. "A ghost? What do you mean?"

"You died a hundred years ago!" I shouted. "I read it in 'Little-Known Victorian Verse!' "

"Hrrumph!" said Twistleton-Tharpe. He began to edge towards me again. "So that's where you got it from! I'm not a ghost!"

"Then what about the crypt?" I quavered. I could feel myself beginning to slide downwards.

"Oh – was that you?" said Twistleton-Tharpe. "I wondered."

The branch gave another crack and I could feel myself going. Twistleton-Tharpe leaned forward. He spoke slowly and distinctly. "I – am – not – a – ghost!" he said. "Hold out your arm."

And just as the branch parted company with the tree I did as he said and hung on to him as hard as

I could. His arm felt strong and muscly – not like a ghost's at all. I was left dangling in mid-air.

Below me I heard the branch hit the rocks and go crashing on down to the bottom of the quarry.

"Don't look!" said Twistleton-Tharpe and he began to haul me in. He lugged me onto what remained of the branch and helped me back to the ground.

We sat together at the foot of the tree without speaking. I looked at Alexander Twistleton-Tharpe. He really **was** as white as a ghost now. I supposed I was, too.

At last Twistleton-Tharpe spoke.

"Let's walk back," he said. "You and I, Josh, have a lot of explaining to do."

. . . . . . . . . . . . .

At first, we walked in silence. From the high path we could see the Abbey and little figures running around the football pitch like ants.

We slid down the hill and it was only when we reached the lakeside that Twistleton-Tharpe spoke again.

"So you thought I was a ghost?" he said.

"You looked like the bloke in 'Victorian Verse' ", I blurted out. "And you've got the same name."

"Didn't you come to my introduction talk in the Great Hall?" asked Twistleton-Tharpe, looking puzzled.

"I ran out," I muttered.

"Aha! That would explain it," said Twistleton-Tharpe. "If you'd stayed to hear my talk, Josh, you'd have known that Alexander Twistleton-Tharpe was my great-great-great grandfather."

I stared.

"But you look just like him," I said.

"It's for publicity purposes – that's all," said Twistleton-Tharpe. "The old boy's got quite an appreciation society, you know, and I often get asked to give talks about him – the beard and the glasses go down rather well."

"Oh!" I said.

"And all first sons in our family are called

Alexander," said Twistleton-Tharpe. "It's a tradition."

We walked on round the lake and I thought over what Twistleton-Tharpe was telling me.

"But what about the crypt?" I burst out. "You **looked** like a ghost. And you couldn't have got through the door – it was chained up."

"Ah, the door!" said Twistleton-Tharpe.

"I could only just manage it," I said. "And I'm much smaller than you."

"There's another door," said Twistleton-Tharpe. "Right behind old Twistleton's headstone. And a passageway that leads down from the Great Hall. It's not used very often – the door's a bit stiff."

Oh. So that explained the creaking.

"But what's his tomb doing in the crypt?" I asked.

"He taught here – for years!" said Twistleton-Tharpe. "Didn't you know? He couldn't live off his poetry – no-one wanted to read it. This place was like home to him – he asked to be buried here."

"But I still don't understand," I said. "What were you doing down there in the middle of the night?"

"I could ask the same about you," said Twistleton-Tharpe, smiling. "Well, if you really want to know,

I'm writing a book about him and I wanted some photos of his headstone – I thought some night shots would be rather effective."

Things were beginning to fall into place.

"I was really scared," I said.

"**You** were scared!" said Twistleton-Tharpe. "What about me? You almost gave me a heart attack. I'd just realised the lights weren't working when you shone that torch at me – I thought **you** were a ghost!"

We were walking up the slope to the wood and Twistleton-Tharpe told me how he'd had to plough through every single word of his great-great-great-grandad's poetry for his book. "And that's why I recognized 'The Lonely Zebra' immediately I saw it," he said. "I thought it was a good send-up of the Zephyr Poem – it really made me laugh."

He paused for breath.

"You've missed quite a lot of my poetry course," he said.

"I'm sorry," I mumbled.

And then Twistleton-Tharpe started talking to me about poetry. He wanted to know how I'd come across 'The Roaming Zephyr' and why I'd done it.

So I explained.

"You see," I ended. "I'm no good at poetry. I really wanted to do football."

"Aha!" said Twistleton-Tharpe.

"I suppose you're going to tell on me?" I said.

Twistleton-Tharpe stroked his beard.

"No," he said at last. "I don't think so. Not if you agree to come to my last workshop."

"Alright!" I said; and a great wave of relief washed over me. We went on talking as we walked through the wood and I learned quite a lot of things. I learned, for instance, that a zephyr is not an animal at all, but a breeze. And I also learned that poetry doesn't have to rhyme.

"It's all about finding the right words," said Twistleton-Tharpe. "The right words for the job."

He recited one or two of his poems to me and I

could tell why the others had laughed – they were really funny, nothing like the older Twistleton-Tharpe's. They were about football and school and skateboarding.

"I try them out on my own children," said Twistleton-Tharpe. "If they laugh I know I'm on the right track."

We reached the edge of the wood.

"You know," said Twistleton-Tharpe, "everyone's good at something. And if they're good at one thing, that usually means they're good at other things, too."

"But I'm no good at poetry," I said. "And I didn't get on to the football."

"You can practice your football," said Twistleton-Tharpe. "And I'm willing to bet we'll get at least one poem out of you before you leave."

He paused.

"But I think we've already found the thing you're good at," he said. "Just leave it with me."

# Chapter 19

I went to the workshop. And I really got stuck into a poem, too. I decided to call it 'Scared Stiff'. It was about roots growing down from your feet and about falling into crocodile pits. It was about shadows and creakings and cold hands on your shoulders. I couldn't stop writing.

I even got up early the next morning to finish it. The footballers were getting up, too, and I could hear their scissors snipping away as they cut their track suit-bottoms into shorts.

Edward had become very popular all of a sudden.

"Here, Ed, give us a lend of your tights!" begged

footballer after footballer; but Edward snuggled under his duvet and didn't answer.

. . . . . . . . . . . . .

So Performance Day was here; and here we were, waiting on the touchline for the first event – the big football match.

There was a gasp as the footballers ran onto the pitch.

They'd all had their heads shaved – even the girls – and they'd each got a felt-tip football drawn on top.

Mr Poole tore at his own hair in despair.

"What are their parents going to say?" I heard him ask Miss Wilson.

Marvin nudged me.

"They went into town," he whispered. "To Colin

the Crimpers. He did them a special deal."

Wayne Boxall was the referee. He wore purple flares and a chunky necklace; he also had long, green dread-locks that he kept flicking back over his shoulders.

"Do you think it's a wig?" said Marvin.

Wayne Boxall blew his whistle and they were off. It was a good match. Kevin scored two goals and his side won by six goals to one. Rob Riley was in goal for the other side and he let in all six of the winning goals. So it was a good result. We had an early lunch and then followed the drama group round as they performed a play they'd written themselves. It was called 'Murder in the Abbey'. It took place in the cloisters, the Great Hall, the rose garden and the wood. Everywhere we went there were dead monks falling from behind pillars and out of trees, clutching their throats and going "Aargh!" It turned out the Abbot did it because he didn't like their singing. It was really good fun.

While the play was going on the teachers got the athletics field set out. There was going to be high jump, long jump, running and javelin. I was just settling down to watch Marvin doing his high-jump when I heard a familiar voice behind me. "Josh – quick! Go and get changed! You're in the cross-country."

I turned and stared at Twistleton-Tharpe.

"It's alright," he said. "I've had a word with Mrs Court."

"But – but – I can't run!" I stuttered.

"No?" said Twistleton-Tharpe. "What about that run yesterday? I've never seen such a turn of speed in a boy of your age. You moved like a rocket."

I gaped at him.

"Go on," said Twistleton-Tharpe. "You can do it." He lowered his voice. "Just pretend you've got a ghost after you," he said.

So that's how I came to be lining up at the start of the cross-country race along with about twenty other kids. The starting-gun cracked and we were away. We went round and round the Sports Field and then into the wood; the track was clearly marked with posts and white tape and there were teachers standing along the route urging us on.

"Come on, Josh!" yelled Mr Poole as we hared along under the trees.

We burst out of the wood and ran down the slope. I was near the front – in fact, I was doing so well I surprised myself. We went round the lake and up the hill. When we reached the top we turned left and ran back towards the wood. It was strange, but it didn't seem at all creepy in there today. Birds were singing and buds were bursting. I felt full of life, too.

"Josh! You can do it!" screamed Miss Wilson, who had appeared next to Mr Poole. They seemed to be holding hands; but I was going so fast I hardly noticed. I tore past them and shot out of the wood.

There was only one runner ahead of me now – a girl with big, muscly legs. I took a deep breath

and I imagined the ghost of Twistleton-Tharpe reaching out to grab me. I accelerated. I ran as I've never run before. I broke the tape with the cheers of the crowd in my ears and collapsed on the ground.

"Well done, Josh!" I could hear Twistleton-Tharpe saying. "I knew you could do it."

"Josh, you were brilliant!" cried Kev, slapping me

on the back. "I didn't know you could run."

"Neither did I!" I panted.

I couldn't believe I'd done it. And I was so elated, that when we had the poetry reading that evening, I didn't hang back like I had in class. I just got up and read my poem and everyone clapped. It was a really good feeling.

I'd already surprised myself twice that day; but there was an even bigger surprise in store – for all of us.

It happened during the Dancing Display. The music struck up and the red curtains opened with a swish.

"Now we get to see Edward in his tights," whispered Kev.

I must admit I was interested. We all leaned forward.

A lot of little girls in white tutus danced on,

pretending to be swans. No sign of Edward. After this there was a tap-dance, with kids dressed in clown's outfits. Still no sign of Edward.

"He must have chickened out," said Barney and we clapped as the last of the clowns pranced off the stage.

There was a drum-roll and some really funky music started up. A spotlight hit the centre of the stage. Into the pool of light leaped a figure in baggy trousers, trainers and a back-to-front baseball cap.

We all stared, open-mouthed.

"It's Edward!" said Barney.

And, sure enough, it was! Edward was the most amazing break-dancer I've ever seen in my life. There was nothing he couldn't do.

He twirled, he leaped, he did hand-springs and he spun round and round on his shoulders.The audience went wild. By the time Edward back-flipped off the stage we were all on our feet, cheering and stamping.

Edward's break-dance brought Performance Day to an end; and I can honestly say that it was the best day I've ever had in my life.

# Chapter 20

Well – that's about it, really. I never thought I'd mind leaving Grimblethorpe Abbey, but I did. It was all because of that last day. Now it was Friday morning, and as our mini-bus neared the pineapple gates I looked back at the spires and felt a twinge of sadness. But it only lasted a moment, because we had such a brilliant time on the way home.

For a start, Miss Wilson and Mr Poole seemed really happy. They kept smiling at each other and didn't seem to notice us at all – which was just as well, because we were making a bit of a racket. Everyone was talking non-stop.

Alicia had lost all interest in me and was sitting

next to Lydia. They were giggling like mad and making friendship bracelets for each other.

Marvin sat next to Edward and I could hear him asking questions about break-dancing. And – surprise, surprise! – Edward was actually answering.

As for me, Kev and Barney, we sat on the back seat and talked about football.

"It was great meeting Wayne Boxall," said Kev.

"Yeah," I said. "But he was a bit of a fashion victim, wasn't he?"

Barney poked me in the ribs.

"Oi!" he said. "That's just because you didn't get to talk to him."

"I did!" I protested. "Well, he spoke to **me**, anyway."

"What did he say?" asked Barney.

"He said 'You! Off!' " said Kev; and we all fell about laughing.

There was a little group of parents waiting at the school gates. We piled out of the mini-bus with our rucksacks and Kevin and Barney's Mums burst into tears.

"What have they done to you?" they wailed. "What's happened to your hair? You're **bald**!"

Miss Wilson tried to pacify them.

"We're really sorry," she said. "They gave us the slip."

"If it's any consolation, there's another twenty just like them," said Mr Poole. "We did get them to wash the footballs off, though," he added as an afterthought.

Mum was waiting with Izzie. Izzie and I rushed at each other and hugged; then we remembered ourselves and sprang apart and glared at each other.

"How did you get on?" asked Mum.

"Josh was brilliant!" said Kevin.

"Oh, good!" said Mum.

"He won the cross-country!" said Barney.

Mum looked puzzled. "What about the poetry?" she asked.

"Oh – that was alright, too," I said.

"Come and sign up for the athletics club after Easter," said Mr Poole, clapping me on the shoulder as he passed by.

Izzie was still glaring at me.

"And what about the ghosts?" she asked. "I bet you were scared, weren't you? How was the headless monk?"

"I didn't see him," I said.

Barney overheard.

"Josh knows how to deal with ghosts, don't you worry," he said. "He was a real hero."

. . . . . . . . . . . . .

"How's the band, Bella?" I asked as we set out for home. I thought I might as well make an effort.

Izzie's reaction was startling.

"Don't call me that!" she yelled and she flounced away up the road ahead of us.

"What's the matter with her?" I asked.

"Ssh!" said Mum. "It's a sore point. The others have thrown her out of the band. They said she was too bossy."

"Oh," I said and we walked along in silence for a while.

"What's that?" asked Mum, nodding at the book I was carrying. She took it and opened it up. " 'Rocket-ships and Roller-blades," she read. " 'By Alexander Twistleton-Tharpe'."

"He was our poetry tutor," I said. "He gave us all a copy – it's really good."

"Oh – he's signed it," said Mum. "And he's written something underneath. 'Keep running, Josh. From the Ghost-Writer'. What does he mean?"

"Dunno," I said. "It could mean a lot of things – you know what poets are like."

And I ran off along the road to catch up with Izzie.